S0-AQC-892

Chocolate! Chocolate! Chocolate!

The Complete Book of Chocolate

SCHOLASTIC INC.
New York Toronto London Auckland Sydney

ISBN 0-590-42155-7

12 11 10 9 8 7 6 5 4 3 2 1   9/8 0 1 2 3 4/9

Printed in the U.S.A.   28

First Scholastic printing, March 1989

Chocolate!
Chocolate! Chocolate!

The Complete Book of Chocolate

CONTENTS

The History of Chocolate

If you're a chocolate lover, it's impossible to imagine a world without chocolate. But, believe it or not, chocolate was one of the deepest, darkest, most deliciously kept secrets until 1492!

When Christopher Columbus returned triumphantly from America he laid before Spain's King Ferdinand and Queen Isabella chests full of strange and wonderful things. Hidden among the treasures were a few dark brown beans that looked like almonds. No one really knew what they were or what to do with them. They were cacao beans (pronounced kə kā′ ō), the source of all our chocolate and cacao! Unfortunately, Chris didn't bring back a chocolate recipe from America so Europeans were forced to wait another twenty-seven years before they could sample this tasty treat.

In 1519 the Spanish explorer Hernando Cortez traveled to Mexico where he found the Aztec Indians using cacao beans in the preparation of the royal drink *chocolatl*. Legend has it that the great Aztec Emperor Montezuma loved the bitter beverage so much he drank fifty golden gobletfuls every day! Montezuma gave Cortez the recipe and some cacao and vanilla beans. Cortez took them back to Spain where the recipe went through a lot of changes. The Spanish king and queen quickly improved the drink by adding sugar and serving it hot.

For the next hundred years the Spanish couldn't bear to share this delicious drink with the rest of Europe. But once the secret leaked out, rich Europeans couldn't get enough of it. Soon the upper classes in most European capitals were sipping hot chocolate. In fact, by the 1700s chocolate was so popular people would go to "chocolate houses" to drink all the chocolate they wanted. And they drank a lot! They believed that chocolate was very good for their looks and health.

In 1765 a man named Baker started a chocolate mill near Boston. By this time people had finally figured out how to make powdered cocoa by extracting some of the cocoa butter from the cacao beans and then grinding them up. To make solid chocolate, they reversed this process by adding fat to ground beans. Eventually all of America would be conquered by the wonderfully sweet sensation known as chocolate!

For years chocolate was made by hand but as the demand increased so did the number of machines that were used to make it. Today, you can buy chocolate in many forms, sizes, shapes, and flavors. But the best is still the homemade kind. This book tells you how to use chocolate to create your very own treats. There are recipes for cakes, cookies, candy, and other mouth watering delights. Try one of them when you feel like treating your family and friends or when you're in the mood to make your sweet tooth very happy!

Chocolate Tidbits

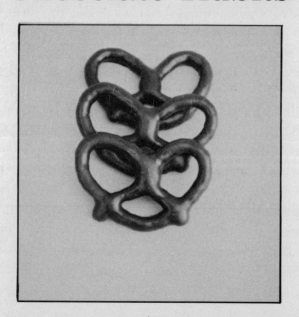

- It takes 400 cacao beans to make one pound of chocolate!
- Chocolate is filled with vitamin A, protein, iron, and vitamin D.
- Some people love chocolate so much that even their spaghetti is chocolate! Martin Johnner, a chef at the Culinary Center of New York, is famous for his "chocolate pasta." It's really very thin chocolate pancakes cut into thin, spaghetti-like strips and topped with whipped cream and chocolate sauce.
- Each year Americans gobble up chocolate at the amazing rate of 15 pounds for every man, woman, and child!
- The world's largest chocolate Easter egg was 17 feet, 9 inches tall and weighed over 2½ tons!
- M&M candies may be M-M good to you, but they were named after their inventors, Forrest Mars and Bruce Murrie.
- To most people the name Hershey means chocolate! But to the people in Pennsylvania it's the home of the famous Hershey chocolate company. The town smells of a different kind of chocolate each day, depending on the type of chocolate being made at the factory!
- When the 3 Musketeers Bar first appeared in 1932 it was divided into three parts — chocolate, vanilla, and strawberry. It wasn't until the 1940's that it became all chocolate and all in one piece.
- The Baby Ruth bar is not named for Babe Ruth the baseball player but for President Grover Cleveland's daughter, Ruth.

- The O'Henry! Bar is not named for the writer O. Henry. It's named after a young man who worked at George Williamson's candy factory. When the women couldn't move the heavy barrels of corn syrup they'd shout, "Oh, Henry!"
- Chocolate chip cookies are the number one best-selling cookies in America. According to the makers of Sunshine cookies, 44 percent of the people who eat chocolate chip cookies like to dunk them.
- A pound of Godiva chocolate sells for $19. It ought to be really rich chocolate, considering a pound of Nestles sells for only $3.

Safety First

Before you jump in and start cooking up a chocolate storm, it would be a good idea for you to read through these cooking tips.

— Check with the grown-ups in your family to find out when the kitchen is free.
— Wear an apron, pull back your hair, and wash your hands before you start.
— Read through the recipe very carefully.
— Before you start, make sure you have all of the ingredients and the proper equipment.
— Be very careful when using the oven or the stove. If you don't feel at ease turning either of them on ask an adult to help you.
— *Important*: Do not try to melt cooking chocolate directly over heat! Place the chocolate pieces in the top part of a double boiler, fill the bottom of the double boiler ¼ full of water. Then heat the double boiler on low heat until the chocolate is completely melted. Another method is to place the chocolate in a small saucepan set in a larger saucepan ¼ full of very hot water.
— Use potholders when taking pans out of the oven or pots off of the stove.
— Wash, dry, and put away all of the utensils. Clean the counters and leave the kitchen clean and neat.
— Check to make sure the oven and stove are off before you leave the kitchen.
— Sit down and enjoy your chocolate creation!

Delicious Chocolate Drinks

Super Ice Cream Soda

(serves 1)

½ cup milk
4 tablespoons chocolate syrup
1 scoop chocolate or vanilla ice cream
club soda or seltzer water

1. Pour the milk and syrup into a tall glass and mix together with a long spoon.
2. Stir in a little club soda or seltzer water.
3. Add the ice cream.
4. Pour in additional club soda or seltzer water to fill the glass.
5. Stir and drink up!

The Basic Shake

(serves 2)

2 cups super cold milk
6 tablespoons chocolate syrup
2 scoops chocolate or vanilla ice cream

1. Use an egg-beater and beat the milk, syrup, and ice cream together in a small mixing bowl.
2. Pour the mixture into two tall glasses.
3. Then try this tasty treat.

The Basic Malt

(serves 2)

2 cups super cold milk
6 tablespoons chocolate syrup
3 scoops chocolate or vanilla ice cream
4 tablespoons malted milk powder*

1. Pour milk, syrup, ice cream, and malted milk powder into a mixing bowl.
2. Beat with an egg-beater.
3. Pour into two tall glasses and enjoy!

* Malt is grain that is softened by being soaked in water and allowed to germinate.

Dynamite Soda-Malt

(serves 1)

3 tablespoons chocolate syrup
3 tablespoons milk
1 cup club soda or seltzer water
1 scoop chocolate ice cream
1 teaspoon malt powder

1. Stir milk and chocolate syrup together in a tall glass.
2. Stir in club soda or seltzer water, then the ice cream.
3. To make it fizz, add more club soda.
4. Sprinkle the top with the malt powder.
5. Get ready for a delightful mouthful.

Eggs-quisite Chocolate Egg Cream

(serves 1)

⅓ cup milk
3 tablespoons chocolate syrup
⅔ cup club soda or seltzer water

1. Pour the milk and chocolate syrup into a tall glass and stir.
2. Slowly stir in the club soda or seltzer water with a long spoon.
3. Then taste this terrific treat.

Originally, egg creams were made with cream and eggs. The modern egg cream uses neither of these ingredients.

Pineappley Frappe

(serves 2)

1½ cups milk
½ cup chocolate syrup or instant chocolate milk mix
½ cup crushed pineapple
4 scoops chocolate ice cream
½ cup club soda

1. Pour milk, syrup or chocolate milk mix, crushed pineapple, and 2 scoops of ice cream into blender or covered container.
2. Blend or shake until mixed well.
3. Put 1 scoop of ice cream into each of two tall glasses.
4. Pour mixture into glasses until about ¾ full.
5. Fill up with club soda.
6. Stir it up and slurp it up!

Choco-Minty Mouthful

(serves 1)

1 cup milk
5 small chocolate-covered mint patties
2 scoops chocolate ice cream

1. Put milk and mint patties into a blender and blend.
2. Add ice cream and blend again.
3. Sip up for a really cool taste.

Tutti-Frutti Warm-Up

(serves 1)

1 cup milk
¼ cup chocolate syrup or instant cocoa mix
1 scoop chocolate or vanilla ice cream
1 teaspoon shredded coconut
1 teaspoon crushed pineapple
miniature marshmallows

1. Pour milk into a saucepan on stove set at low heat to warm. Be careful that it doesn't scorch.
2. Place syrup or cocoa mix into mug.
3. Pour warm milk into mug and stir.
4. Add marshmallows.
5. Top with ice cream.
6. Sprinkle on coconut and crushed pineapple.
7. Dig in!

Peanutty Chocolate Pleaser

(serves 1)

1 cup milk
2 tablespoons peanut butter
¼ cup chocolate syrup or instant cocoa mix
whipped cream
chopped peanuts

1. Pour milk into a saucepan on stove set at low heat to warm. Watch carefully, so that the milk doesn't scorch.
2. Place peanut butter and chocolate syrup or instant cocoa into a mug.
3. Pour warm milk into a mug and stir.
4. Top with whipped cream and sprinkle on nuts.
5. Grab a spoon and spoon up this delicious warm drink!

Slush-ous Chocolate Ice

(serves 4)

1 package instant chocolate pudding
2 cups ice

1. Mix pudding according to directions on the package.
2. Pour mixture into ice cube trays and freeze.
3. When frozen, remove from freezer and put pudding cubes into a blender.
4. Add the two cups of ice.
5. Blend.
6. When the mixture turns into a luscious slush, pour into glasses and serve. Mmmm, mmmm, good!

Cookies, Cakes, and Other Goodies

Blissful, Kiss-ful Cookies

1 cup butter or margarine
½ cup granulated sugar
½ cup brown sugar (packed)
2 eggs

1½ teaspoons vanilla
2¾ cups all-purpose flour
½ teaspoon baking soda
1 teaspoon salt
1 large bag of chocolate kisses

1. Preheat oven to 400°.
2. Mix butter or margarine, both sugars, eggs, and vanilla thoroughly.
3. In a separate bowl, mix the flour, baking soda, and salt.
4. Add the dry ingredients to the margarine mixture.
5. Now mix everything together again — with your hands. (Wash them first!) This is a good way to make sure all the ingredients are completely mixed.
6. Press and mold the dough into a long, smooth roll that's about 2½ inches wide.

7. Wrap in waxed paper and put it in the refrigerator for several hours or overnight.
8. Slice the dough into ¼ inch thick rounds and place them on an ungreased cookie sheet.
9. Place one chocolate kiss on top of each cookie round. Then cover the kiss with another slice of cookie dough.
10. Use a fork to pinch the edges closed.
11. Bake the cookies in the preheated oven for about 8 minutes or until they are lightly browned.
12. Wait until they have cooled before removing them from the sheet and slipping them into your mouth!

Ting-a-lings!

1 12 ounce bag of chocolate chips
1 5 ounce can of chow mein noodles

1. Put the chocolate chips into the top of a double boiler. Set the boiler over very low heat. Stir the chocolate chips until they are melted.
2. Pour the chow mein noodles into the chocolate mixture and stir until all the noodles are completely covered with chocolate.
3. Drop teaspoonfuls of the mixture onto a waxed, paper-lined tray and place them in the refrigerator to harden.
4. When they become hard, remove Ting-a-lings from the refrigerator and enjoy! They should be stored in a cool place.

What a Chunk of Chocolate!

2 bars (6½ ounces each) milk chocolate
1 cup seedless raisins
1 cup miniature marshmallows
½ cup chopped walnuts

1. Break the chocolate up and put it into the top of a double boiler. Set the double boiler over very, very low heat. The water in the bottom of the boiler must never get really hot. Just keep it warm.
2. Stir the chocolate until melted. Add the raisins, marshmallows, and walnuts.
3. Drop teaspoonfuls of the mixture onto a waxed, paper-lined tray. Place in the refrigerator to harden.
4. Once they've solidified, help yourself.

Frosted Pretzels

1 can (16½ ounces) chocolate frosting
15 small pretzel twists

1. Measure 1 cup frosting.
2. Heat the 1 cup of frosting in top of double boiler over hot water until frosting is liquid, stirring occasionally. Remove from heat. Keep the top of the double boiler over the hot water.
3. Carefully dip the pretzels into the frosting with your fingers. Place them on waxed paper. Let dry for 8 hours.

Rocky Road Fudge

¼ cup milk
2 packages (5¾ ounces each) milk chocolate chips
2 cups miniature marshmallows
½ cup chopped nuts

1. Grease a square baking pan, 8 × 8 × 2 inches, with some butter or margarine.
2. Heat ¼ cup of milk and the chocolate chips in a saucepan over low heat until chocolate chips melt, stirring constantly.
3. Remove from heat. Stir in the 2 cups miniature marshmallows and ½ cup chopped nuts. The marshmallows will make little lumps in the candy.
4. Spread the candy in the buttered pan with a spatula. Refrigerate about 1 hour or until firm. Cut into 1-inch squares.

Popular Chocolate Pops

1 package of instant chocolate pudding
3½ cups of milk
¼ cup of sugar
toothpicks

1. Follow the directions on the package of pudding, but add the extra milk and sugar. The chocolate will be thinner than regular pudding.
2. Pour the mixture into Popsicle molds or into ice-cube trays.
3. Put plastic wrap over the top and carefully punch toothpicks into each cube.
4. Freeze!

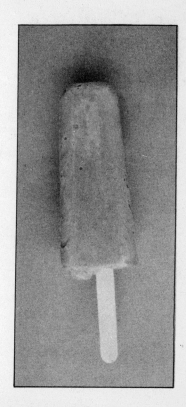

More Than an Instant Chocolate Pudding

2 cups milk in a large pan (separate from the other ingredients)
3 tablespoons cornstarch
½ cup sugar

¼ teaspoon salt
¼ cup milk (separate from the other milk)
5 tablespoons cocoa powder

---

1. Heat the two cups of milk in the pan over a low flame.
2. Meanwhile, mix the cornstarch, sugar, salt, and ¼ cup milk in a mixing bowl. Mix these ingredients until there are no lumps. (This is important!)
3. When the two cups of milk are hot, add the five tablespoons of cocoa. (Do not try to put cocoa into the milk when the milk is cold — it won't mix.) Stir until the cocoa and milk are mixed.

4. Add the ingredients from the mixing bowl to the hot milk and cocoa.
5. Keep everything over a low flame. Stir, stir, stir! Don't let any cocoa stick to the bottom of the pan. When the milk is hot enough, your pudding will thicken.
6. Pour thickened pudding into bowls, and put the bowls into the refrigerator and allow to set for two hours.

Take a Break Chocolate Candy

1 12-ounce package of semisweet chocolate chips
8 1.65-ounce plain chocolate bars

16 large marshmallows, cut up small
1 cup of your favorite nuts

---

1. Put the chips and broken-up chocolate bars into the top of a double boiler. Melt them and mix them together over a low flame.
2. When they are melted, remove the top pan of the double boiler and add the marshmallow pieces and nuts to the melted mix. Mix everything together well.

3. Pour the mix into a well-greased 8½ inch square cake pan. Put the pan in the refrigerator and let the candy cool.
4. When the candy is hard, break into chunks, and serve it up!

Chocolate Leaves

20 real leaves
1 teaspoon butter
2 ounces baking chocolate (either sweet or
semi-sweet, whichever you like)

---

1. Go outside and gather leaves. Yes, leaves! Rose leaves, mint leaves, tree leaves (maple leaves are very nice). (Be careful not to pick poison ivy!) Don't use dead leaves, though — green ones only.

2. Wash your leaves thoroughly under cold water. Dry them between two paper towels. Put them on a cookie sheet.

3. Put the butter and baker's chocolate into the top of a double boiler and melt them, mixing them together into a paste.

4. Using a butter knife, spread the chocolate paste onto the *bottoms* of the leaves, about ¼ inch thick or thicker. Put the chocolate-covered leaves back on the cookie sheet, chocolate side up.

5. Put the cookie sheet into the refrigerator or freezer. When the chocolate is hard, take the sheet out and carefully peel the leaves away from the chocolate.

6. Your chocolate leaves can either be eaten as a candy, or used as cake decorations.

Super Easy Never Fail Chocolate Cake

3 cups flour
2 cups sugar
⅔ cup cocoa powder
2 teaspoons baking soda
1 teaspoon salt

2 cups water
⅔ cup vegetable oil
2 teaspoons vanilla extract
2 teaspoons white vinegar

---

1. Preheat oven to 350 degrees.
2. Put all the dry ingredients together in a large bowl — that's the flour, sugar, cocoa, baking soda, and salt. Mix well.
3. Add all the other ingredients to the same bowl. Mix everything very well.
4. Pour your batter into either two 9-inch layer pans for a double-decker cake, or one 9 × 13-inch pan. You don't need to grease the pans.

5. Pop the pan or pans into the oven, and bake for about 30 minutes or until a knife put into the middle of the cake comes out clean.
6. When the cake is done, let it cool for 20 minutes, cut, and eat!

Plain Old Chocolate Frosting

(Frosts two 9-inch cake layers)

4 squares unsweetened chocolate
1 cup sifted confectioners' sugar
3 tablespoons hot tap water

1 egg
4 tablespoons butter or margarine

---

1. Drop the chocolate into the top of a double boiler and melt it over hot, but not boiling, water. Stir occasionally with a long spoon.
2. When the chocolate is melted, turn off the stove and carefully lift off the top of the double boiler. Let chocolate cool for a minute.
3. Add the sugar and 3 tablespoons of hot water to the melted chocolate. Beat with a mixing spoon.

4. Break the egg into a cup and mix it with a fork. Then add it to the chocolate mixture. Beat well.
5. Add the butter or margarine, a tablespoon at a time, and beat until the frosting is smooth and creamy.
6. Spread on cake that has cooled.

Delicious Brownies

4 ounces unsweetened chocolate
⅔ cup shortening
2 cups granulated sugar
4 eggs
1 teaspoon vanilla

1¼ cups all-purpose flour*
1 teaspoon baking powder
1 teaspoon salt
1 cup chopped nuts

---

1. Heat the oven to 350 degrees. Grease a 13 × 9 × 2-inch baking pan with shortening.
2. Heat chocolate and shortening in saucepan over low heat until the chocolate melts. Remove from heat. Mix in sugar, eggs, and vanilla. Stir in flour, baking powder, salt, and chopped nuts. Spread the batter in the greased pan.

3. Bake for 30 minutes or until the brownies start to pull away from the sides of the pan.
4. Cool and cut into bars.

* If using self-rising flour, omit the baking powder and salt.

Have a Chocolate Party

Now that you've got this incredible collection of delicious chocolate recipes, don't keep them all to yourself. Share them with your friends. Invite the gang over for great games and tasty treats at a chock-full-of-fun Chocolate Party! Here's everything you need to know to throw a super-sweet chocolate celebration.

PARTY PREPARATIONS

Date: Once you decide to have a Chocolate Party there are a lot of things that have to be done. The first thing you have to do is pick a date and time for your party. Avoid choosing dates that fall on holidays, as families generally have plans to do things together, and you want everyone you invite to be able to attend your party. Also, check with your parents to make sure they'll be home to supervise and give you a hand during your party. If for some reason they can't be there, ask an adult relative or friend to help you out.

There's one more thing to keep in mind when you pick your party date: You should give yourself lots of time to really prepare for the party. Pick a date that is at least four weeks away. Then send out your invitations at least two weeks in advance. This way your guests will have plenty of time to prepare *themselves* for your big affair.

Invitations: Invitations that you make yourself can be truly special. So gather your artistic talents and artistic materials: sheets of oak tag or construction paper, (brown, preferably), crayons, watercolors, magic markers, glue, glitter, etc., and design a super-special invitation for this big occasion.

To get started with your invitation, first take a sheet of paper and fold it down the middle. Then fold it in the middle once again. The folded paper will look like a regular greeting card. On the face of the card you can draw assorted chocolate candy goodies or cut out chocolate goodies from magazines and paste them on for a real chocolate-covered card. Afterward, glue on your glitter for added sparkle.

On the inside of the card, make sure you write down the date of the party, the place, and the time. You should also include your telephone number and the letters R.S.V.P. so your friends will call to let you know if they'll be able to attend the party.

For another great invitation idea try this. You'll need oak tag paper and wrappers from chocolate bars. Write out the party information (date, time, place) on each sheet of paper. Then fold up the paper and slip it *inside* the chocolate candy wrapper! You can think up other ideas to make your invitations as exciting as your Chocolate Party.

Dress: This will probably be the first time your friends have ever been invited to a *Chocolate* Party. So one question they'll most likely ask is, "What do I wear to a Chocolate Party?" Well, if they happen to have pieces of clothing with chocolate designs (chocolate fudge, chocolate kisses, ice cream cones, etc.) that's perfect. Otherwise they can wear something old, or something new, or something borrowed but definitely something *brown*! The entire outfit can be brown — or just part of the outfit. It could be a brown hat, brown socks, brown shoes, brown bow tie, brown hair ribbons, brown pants, brown skirt — get the picture?

Decorations: The night before or the morning of the party is a good time to decorate. Whether it's in your living room, den, basement, attic, or garage, these decorating tips are terrific:
1. What's a party without balloons! Instead of just hanging up plain balloons, you can tie little chocolate bars onto the balloon strings.
2. String chocolate kisses on threads to hang across the ceiling or wall.

You can even roll up aluminum foil to *look* like chocolate kisses and string those along the walls or ceiling instead of the real thing.

3. Cut out pictures of chocolate goodies such as cakes, cookies, fudge, etc. Paste them together collage-style on construction paper. Hang your chocolatey collages on the walls around your party room.

4. String chocolate candy wrappers together and hang across walls or ceiling.

Activities: Here are all kinds of fun games you can play to make your Chocolate Party chock-full of fun!

1. To get your guests to mix and mingle right from the start, try this. As guests arrive, hand each one a half of a chocolate candy or chocolate goody (i.e., chocolate brownie, chocolate chip cookie, Reese's Peanut Butter Cup, Hershey's Chocolate, etc.). Eventually, each of your guests should be holding half of a particular piece of chocolate "something." What they have to do then is to try to find the person who is holding the *other* matching half to their chocolate goody. And in the meantime, everyone will be having a good time getting to know each other during their "sweets" search!

2. You've played Pin-the-Tail-on-the-Donkey, for sure. But have you ever played Pin-the-Tail-on-the-Chocolate-Bunny? Bet you haven't. Well, there's a first time for everything. And the first time you play this game you're sure to discover it's a lot of fun. Before you can play, however, you have to make your chocolate bunny. So, draw a big bunny on brown construction paper or color in a brown bunny on plain white paper. On a separate sheet of paper draw and cut out several bunny tails — one for each player (you can make them bigger than a regular bunny's tail — just for this game). Tape up the bunny on a wall. As in Pin-the-Tail-on-the-Donkey, players in this game are also blindfolded, and spun around before they attempt to pin the tail on the bunny.

3. Guessing games are always good. Fill up a jar with M&Ms and have your party guests try to guess how many M&Ms are in the jar. Winner takes all, of course!

4. A good game of hide and seek is lots of fun. But it's double the fun when you play hide and seek with foil-covered chocolate coins. Hide the chocolate coins all over the party room. Keep track of how many are hidden and have guests try to find them all. Finder's keepers!

5. Here's a guessing game chocolate lovers will absolutely love. Write

the names of various chocolate-related things on pieces of paper. Write words such as: Milton Hershey, Hershey Park, chocolate-chip cookies, chocolate fudge, M&Ms, chocolate syrup, chocolate frosting, chocolate-covered raisins, chocolate-covered almonds, Snickers, Reese's Peanut Butter Cups, "Charlie and the Chocolate Factory," and so on. . . . Place the pieces of paper inside a paper bag. Have players pick pieces of paper at random, then *describe* the chocolate "thing" for others to figure out.

6. Here's a game of jigsaw you never saw before! This is the game plan. First, you'll need two large pieces of cardboard (from a big gift box, for example). On each piece of cardboard draw a big chocolate cake or giant chocolate ice cream cone, or some other chocolate food. Both pictures must be of the *same* "thing." Once you're done — cut up the drawings! Yes, cut them up. No, not in tiny pieces. Just make definite cuts so that each picture can be put back together again. Each drawing should be cut into the same amount of puzzle pieces. Now, on with the game. Form two teams with an equal number of players. Pile the puzzle pieces in two separate piles at the front of the room. The two teams should form lines facing their puzzle pieces — but a good distance away. At the signal (someone says, "On your marks, get set, go!") the first one in line on each team runs to their pile and picks up

one piece of the puzzle and returns to the team, placing the puzzle piece on the floor. The next player in line repeats the same action, after the preceding player has returned to the starting spot. The faster a player is, the better for the team. Once all the pieces of the puzzle are gathered up, the teammates *all* try to put the jigsaw puzzle back together again. The team that does this first is the winner.

7. You'll raise a lot of laughs with this chocolate-covered raisin game. Divide the guests into two teams. Each team forms a line. Each team should be given one plastic spoon and an equal amount of chocolate-covered raisins, plus a small bowl. The teams then place their raisins on a table at one end of the room and the bowl at the other end of the room. The object is for the first person in line to pick up one raisin with the plastic spoon — using one hand only! — race over to the bowl at the other end of the room, drop the raisin in, and race back. The next person takes the spoon and the race continues until one team gets all their raisins into the bowl.

Party Planning Lists

Here is a list of lists to help you prepare for your party from the beginning planning stages up to party time!

PARTY GUEST LIST

Name	Telephone	Response
1. _____	_____	yes ____ no ____
2. _____	_____	yes ____ no ____
3. _____	_____	yes ____ no ____
4. _____	_____	yes ____ no ____
5. _____	_____	yes ____ no ____
6. _____	_____	yes ____ no ____
7. _____	_____	yes ____ no ____
8. _____	_____	yes ____ no ____

9. _____ _____ yes ____ no ____

10. _____ _____ yes ____ no ____

11. _____ _____ yes ____ no ____

12. _____ _____ yes ____ no ____

13. _____ _____ yes ____ no ____

14. _____ _____ yes ____ no ____

15. _____ _____ yes ____ no ____

16. _____ _____ yes ____ no ____

17. _____ _____ yes ____ no ____

18. _____ _____ yes ____ no ____

19. _____ _____ yes ____ no ____

20. _____ _____ yes ____ no ____

PARTY SUPPLIES (for decorations, invitations, refreshments, etc.)

____ paper plates

____ paper cups

____ plastic forks, knives, spoons

____ napkins

____ paper tablecloth

____ balloons

____ string

____ aluminum foil

____ empty chocolate candy wrappers

____ tape

____ thumb tacks

____ crepe paper streamers

____ construction paper

____ magic markers

____ crayons

____ glue

____ old magazines

____ glitter

____

____

Other: _____

PARTY GAMES LIST

1. _____

2. _____

3. _____

4. _____

5. _____

6. _____

7. _____

8. _____

9. _____

10. _____

PARTY MENU (food and drinks)

Snacks:

_____

_____

_____

_____

Drinks:

_____

_____

_____

Other:

_____

FINAL PARTY PLANNING CHECK LIST

_____ invitations sent and received

_____ adult supervision chosen

_____ party room chosen

_____ party decorations planned

_____ refreshments planned

_____ supplies (paper plates, cups, spoons, forks, etc.) bought

_____ refreshments prepared

_____ snack tables set up

_____ party decorations put up

_____ game props prepared

_____ party outfit ready

_____ party host or hostess ready

Notes

Use the following pages for notes, recipes, or your own super party
ideas.

Notes